To Finn and Brunhilde

Library of Congress Cataloging-in-
Publication Data available.

ISBN 978-1-4521-6334-5

Manufactured in China.

MIX
Paper from
responsible sources
FSC
www.fsc.org
FSC™ C008047

Design by Ryan Hayes.
Typeset in Sentinel.
The illustrations in this book were
rendered in watercolor and ink.

10 9 8 7 6 5 4 3 2 1

Chronicle Books LLC
680 Second Street
San Francisco, California 94107

Chronicle Books—we see things
differently. Become part of our
community at www.chroniclekids.com.

CYCLE CITY

by Alison Farrell

chronicle books·san francisco

It's morning in Cycle City, and the Parade Committee is a little nervous.

Attn: Mayor Snail
Subject: Last-Minute Invitation List

guest: Etta Elephant
bike: kid tandem
note: Etta will be visiting her
Aunt Ellen

guest: The Bunny Family
bike: super loooooong box bike
note: they will be at a birthday
party

guest: Polar Bear
bike: gelato bike
note: try the bacio gelato,
it's delizioso!

guest: Owl
bike: bookmobile
note: her rounds stop by the
food bikes and the canal

guest: Chickadee
bike: boot bike
note: Chickadee still has some
assembly to do!

guest: Frog
bike: amphibious
note: often seen near water

guest: Hippo
bike: camper bike
note: Hippo will be packing
for a camping trip today

find: Guinea Pig
bike: tall bike
note: Guinea Pig made her own bike!

At the train station, folks are starting their day.
Camp kids head to the playground in a school bus bike. Cardinal hails a
pedicab. Gorilla commutes to work on a hand-cranked bicycle.

"Eureka!" calls Mayor Snail. "I've found Etta Elephant!"
Can you find Etta Elephant?

Downtown, Buffalo delivers tulips with a box bike.
Lemur hurts his long tail. Where is Alpaca off to with that baker bike?

"Hooray, I spy the Bunny family!" says the Mayor.
Can you find the Bunny family?

In the park, the Lovebirds stroll around with a tandem.
Monkey rides an unusual unicycle. Who will the pedicab driver pick up next?

"There's Polar Bear!" announces Mayor Snail.
Where is Polar Bear? Do you see him?

The food bikes are a busy place at lunchtime!
Armadillo hops on a high-wheeled penny-farthing.
Etta orders her favorite food. Where would you eat?

"Yahoo!" cries the Mayor. "I've spotted Owl!"
Can you find Owl?

Next to the food bikes is a nice spot to eat.
Giraffe's special friend waits with vanilla gelato.
The bunnies are at home, mostly napping.
Who was the first Mayor of Cycle City?

"Fancy meeting you here!" says
Mayor Snail to Chickadee.
Can you find Chickadee?

At the canal, Salamander delivers lunch to his friend.
Buffalo goes home to take a break.
The pigs have missed another important piece of parade planning.

"Hold up, Frog!" shouts Mayor Snail.
"I've got something for you!"
Do you see Frog?

Over the bridge, Etta and Ellen shop for costumes.
A flock of birds on a quint tandem say goodbye to their passenger.
Armadillo finds her cycling club.

"Aha, there is Hippo!" says Mayor Snail.
Where is Hippo?

Just before the parade, folks are still practicing their acts.
The Parade Supply store is particularly busy.
An ambulance driver needs room to pass.

"At long last! Guinea Pig!" declares Mayor Snail.
"You are the final citizen on my list!"
Where is Guinea Pig?
Which bike do you think Mayor Snail will ride to the parade?

And who will be Grand Marshal?

LET THE PARADE BEGIN!

AROUND TOWN WHEELS & MORE

GRAND MARSHAL

After the parade, Ellen takes Etta back to
the station to be picked up by Dad . . .

and Mayor Snail finds his way home.

What a wonderful day in Cycle City!

hobby horse
velocipede
draisine

boneshaker
(wood wheels + metal tires=
bumpy ride)

penny-farthing
(named after coins)

tandem

trailer bike

multi-wheel
unicycle

adult seat

kid
seats

triplet tandem
family tandem

recumbent

child seat

quad tandem
family tandem

art bike

tall unicycle
giraffe unicycl

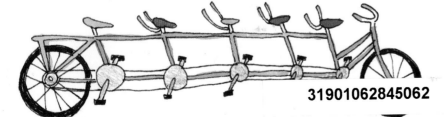

31901062845062

quint tandem

lowrider